Armor of God

By Riley Weber

RileyWeberArt.com

ARMOR OF GOD

RILEY WEBER

"Put on the whole armor of God", the scriptures say.
And be protected from all evil that may come your way.

BELT OF

TRUTH

The belt of truth should be buckled tight.
Truth makes it easy to choose the right.

BREASTPLATE OF

RIGHTEOUSNESS

Don the strong breastplate of righteousness.
With righteousness, temptation is less.

GOSPEL OF

PEACE

The gospel of peace will ground your feet.
The path of the gospel can't be beat.

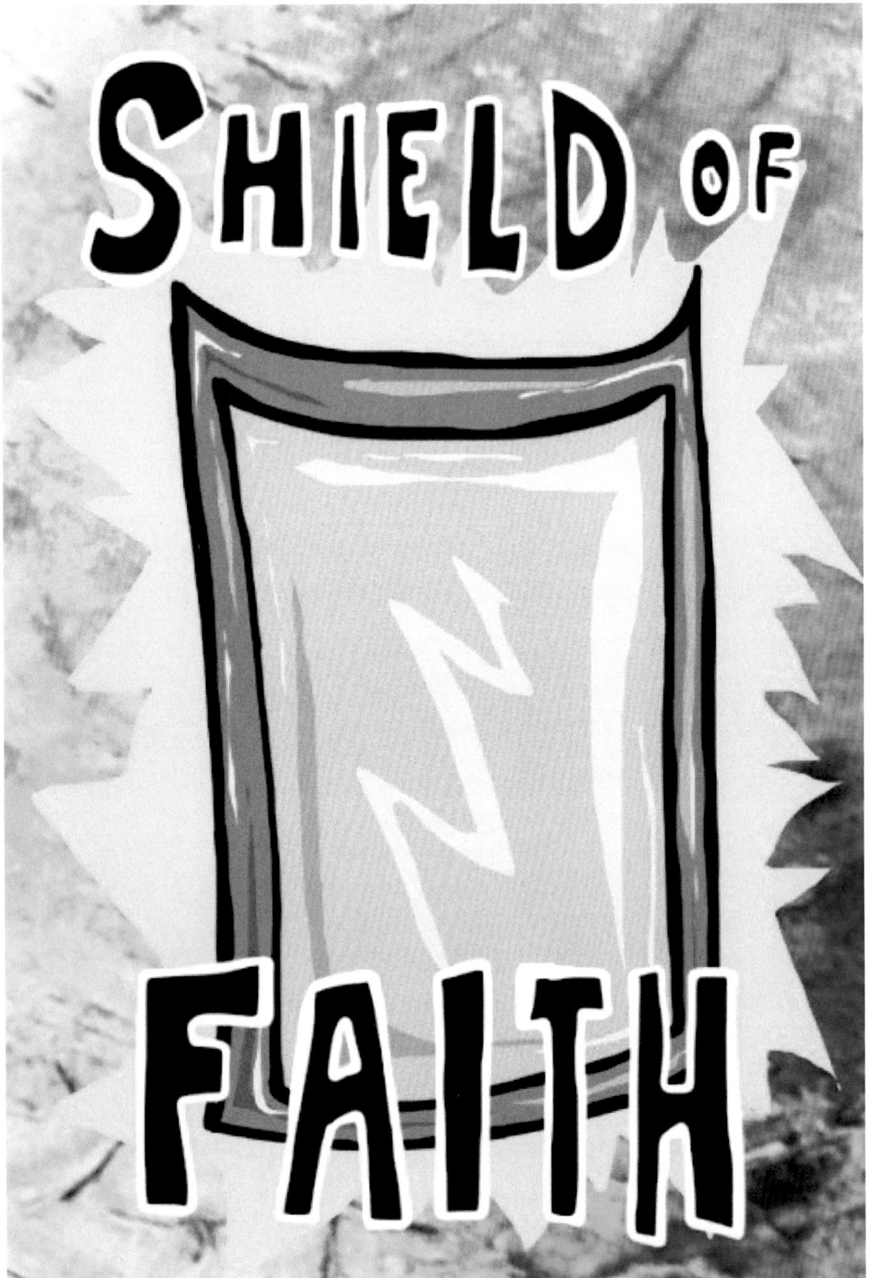
SHIELD OF
FAITH

With the shield of faith in your hand, hold fast.
The shield of faith is a defense to last.

HELMET OF

SALVATION

Atop your head rests the helmet of salvation.
Salvation will keep us from devastation.

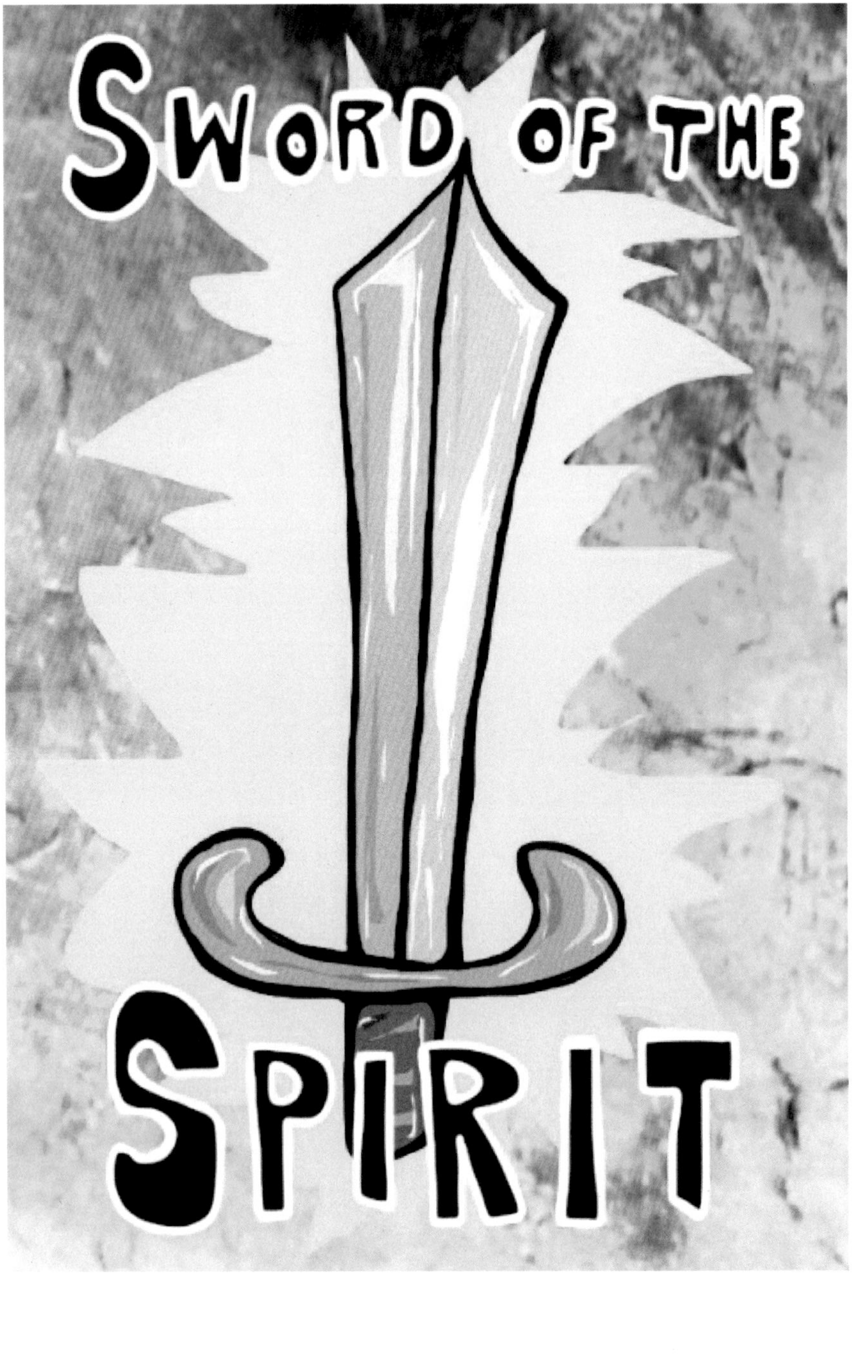
SWORD OF THE
SPIRIT

The sword of the spirit is gripped firmly in hand.
The spirit can help us to make a strong stand.

Stand with your armor all shiny and bright.
Stand with your armor be it day or night.

Life is a marathon and not a quick sprint.
This piece of advice is just a small hint.

Pray to God daily and thank him dutifully.
Remember to ask for his blessings continually.

The wiles of the devil are tricky and sly.
The whole armor of God will keep you ready and spry.

Physical armor protects us on all sides.
Spiritual armor protects us from evil's disguise.

Be sure that your armor is securely in place.
You'll be grateful to know you have God's grace.

Stand with God's armor every day of the year.
(Your name), Stand with God's whole armor and have no fear.

Ephesians 6: 10-18

10 Finally, my brethren, be strong in the Lord, and in the power of his might.

11 Put on the whole armour of God, that ye may be able to stand against the wiles of the devil.

12 For we wrestle not against flesh and blood, but against principalities, against powers, against the rulers of the darkness of this world, against spiritual wickedness in high places.

13 Wherefore take unto you the whole armour of God, that ye may be able to withstand in the evil day, and having done all, to stand.

14 Stand therefore, having your loins girt about with truth, and having on the breastplate of righteousness;

15 And your feet shod with the preparation of the gospel of peace;

16 Above all, taking the shield of faith, wherewith ye shall be able to quench all the fiery darts of the wicked.

17 And take the helmet of salvation, and the sword of the Spirit, which is the word of God:

18 Praying always with all prayer and supplication in the Spirit, and watching thereunto with all perseverance and supplication for all saints;

About the Author

Riley Weber has a strong belief in Christ and all his teachings. Riley wrote this book about the armor of God because he realizes how important it is to fortify ourselves daily against evil and darkness. Every piece of the armor of God is important to put on daily. If, for example, we don't have on the breastplate of righteousness, the Adversary knows it, and may try to attack us there; where we are weakest. The whole armor of God is important for not only kids, but adults as well. With the whole armor of God on, we can then make a strong stand against evil and darkness.

Check out other book titles written and illustrated by Riley Weber. Riley has a unique artistic and writing style. His art is mixed with actual paintings he has done with cartoons he draws on paper and on his tablet. The textured backgrounds add character and personality to each page and his cartoon drawings are vibrant and colorful.

Riley Weber is also a musician (See music by Nooshi). His often lyrical writing style is reflected in his books. Together, his unique artistic and writing style blends into memorable stories for both young and old.

Visit www.rileyweberart.com

Music by Nooshi

Discover Contemporary Pop Children's Music
Composed and Recorded by Riley Weber, a.k.a. Nooshi.

Made in the USA
Columbia, SC
29 November 2018